The Forgotten Ornament

Fulton Books, Inc.
Meadville, PA

Published by Fulton Books 2020

ISBN 978-1-64654-230-7 (paperback)
ISBN 978-1-64654-231-4 (digital)

Printed in the United States of America

The Forgotten Ornament

PEGGY HARP LEE

Snow was falling outside. The warmth of the fireplace glowed against the frosted windowpanes. The turkey was cleared from the table and the discarded wrappings had been gathered and tossed in to the bin.

All that was left of Christmas was the tree.

One by one the ornaments were removed and carefully wrapped and packed away with the anticipation of decorating yet another tree next year!

The boys carried the tree to the backyard, where it leaned against the wooden fence to become a winter home for the small animals of the forest.

But unnoticed, deep between the branches of the now undecorated pine tree, was one lonely toy soldier. He had been forgotten!

He wondered, as he hung shivering in the cold night air, "What happens to the ornaments that are forgotten? Do we become a chew toy for the forest creatures, or do we simply get covered with snow and melt away in the springtime sun? Oh, I certainly hope not!" he cried.

Just as a tear started to roll down his cheek, a beautiful glow of light plucked him from the tree and carried him up into the midnight sky.

"Maybe I am going to be placed on top of the tallest tree in the forest so I can be seen by all."

No, that couldn't happen because if the wind blew really hard, he would fall down…down…down in to the cold snow below.

The beautiful glow carried him past the treetops and into the darkness. "Maybe I will be placed in the sky among the stars!" No, that couldn't happen because he did not shine like the stars, and no one would even know that he was there.

"Oh, where am I going and what will become of me?" the toy soldier worried.

Then just as the worry started to grow inside of him, the sky opened to a sparkling brightness that almost blinded him.

As he looked below, while still in the grasp of the beautiful glow, his eyes began to see something delightful. There stood before him the biggest Christmas tree he had ever seen!

"Where are we?" he asked as he turned to look at the beautiful glow. To his amazement, a dazzling angel was looking back at him.

"Look carefully, dear soldier," she said, her voice sounding like a song. "What do you see? Take your time…look carefully."

As the soldier squinted to make out the tiny movements below him, the angel carried him closer and closer to the objects beneath him.

"Why, it's dogs and cats and horses! These are animals that I remember from where I live! Am I home?"

"No, not at home"—she smiled—"but someplace just as happy. Look carefully, what do you see?"

"They are all decorated with golden collars that have their name shining brightly on them."

"Not just their name," her gentle voice pointed out, "but the name of their person as well."

"But look, over there the dogs and cats and horses don't have collars, but they are with people."

"You have reached the Rainbow Bridge, where all of the animals who have left earth gather on one side around this glorious tree to wait for their person to join them.

"When they meet, they cross the bridge together where the golden collars with shining names are no longer needed."

"What about the homeless and shelter animals that have no person?" asked the toy soldier.

"They are the luckiest of all," sang the angel, "for they get to choose their person from all of the people on earth!"

"Why, this is the grandest place to ever be! To hang among the other forgotten ornaments to welcome the new arrivals and comfort them as they wait for their loved one."

"You are no longer a forgotten ornament," replied the angel as she placed him on the tree. "You are now a remembered ornament, for you will always be remembered by all of the animals who have come to cross this very special bridge. Here you will remain greeting and saying goodbye to the most loved creatures in all of God's heaven—our pets. For only pets love you unconditionally. They love you when you are sad or happy. They love you if you are rich or poor."

"If only people could love that way," the toy soldier responded.

"Then joy and peace and happiness would cover our world forever!"

Then Joy,

and Peace and

happiness would

cover

our world forever

About the Author

Peggy Harp Lee is a first-time children's book author but a long-time reader of all tales delightful to the many children she has encountered in her life. Having graduated in early childhood education from St. Andrews Presbyterian College, she not only read to her second and third grade students on a daily basis but also to her Sunday school classes as well. After becoming a mother of two, and now a grandmother of two, she has continued to read the new and timeless children's stories they have asked for time and time again. She always felt she had a story of her own to tell, and when asked one day by her daughter, Whitney Lee Christensen, "Where do the forgotten ornaments go?" her inspiration was triggered, and her first book was born!

CPSIA information can be obtained
at www.ICGtesting.com
Printed in the USA
LVHW071041061220
673104LV00016B/107